THE

ROYAL

BEE

THE
ROYAL
BEE

by Frances Park and Ginger Park

Illustrations by Christopher Zhong-Yuan Zhang

BOYDS MILLS PRESS

Published by Caroline House
Boyds Mills Press, Inc.
A Highlights Company
815 Church Street
Honesdale, Pennsylvania 18431
Printed in China

Publisher Cataloging-in-Publication Data
Park, Frances.
   The royal bee / by Frances and Ginger Park ; illustrat-
ed by Christopher Zhong-Yuan Zhang.—1st ed.
   [32]p. : col. ill. ;   cm.
Summary: A poor boy from Korea is determined to win
a spelling bee, even though poverty keeps him from for-
mally attending school.
ISBN 1-56397-614-5 hc 1-56397-867-9 pbk
1. Korea - Juvenile fiction. [1. Korea—Fiction.]
I. Park, Ginger. II. Zhang, Christopher Zhong-Yuan, ill.
III. Title.
   [E]—dc21 2000 AC   CIP
Library of Congress Catalog Card Number 98-88234

First edition, 2000
Book design by Amy Drinker, Aster Designs
The text of this book is set in 13—point Leawood Book.
The illustrations are done in oil paints on board.

hc 10 9 8 7 6 5 4 3 2 1
pbk 10 9 8 7 6 5 4 3 2 1

To our grandfather
and to children everywhere.
—F.P. and G.P.

To my daughter, Xing Xin.
—C.Z.Z

AUTHORS' NOTE

The Royal Bee *was inspired by the true
story of our grandfather, Hong Seung Han,
when he was an illiterate boy in late nine-
teenth-century Korea. Too poor to attend
school, he would eavesdrop at the door of
the rich children's schoolhouse until he
was eventually allowed to attend. After he
won a national academic contest, the
Governor of his province invited him to
reside in the palace. There, he tutored the
Governor's young son while continuing
his education.*

*Years later our grandfather
attended seminary in Pyongyang under
the teachings of an American missionary
and became a prominent church minister.
In 1905 he wed our grandmother, Pang
Seung Hwa. Together they became
missionaries in China.*

In the days when kings ruled Korea, only the privileged *yangban* children went to school. They wore fine clothing and carried handsome books. They competed in The Royal Bee at the Governor's palace. They grew up to be scholars and noblemen.

Song-ho was not among the privileged. He was a *sangmin* boy dressed in rags. But the distant sound of a school bell made him dream of the day when he could read books and write poetry.

Song-ho watched his mother wash her tired face in a bowl of water as the meager dawn light worked its way into their small hut. She stood over Song-ho and murmured, "Be good today."

"I will do all my chores," Song-ho promised.

Then she was off into the autumn cornfields.

Song-ho's father had been a fisherman, but he died at sea years ago. Song-ho's mother worked as a farmhand harvesting whatever crop was in season to put food on the table. If she were lucky, she would bring home an armload of wilted fruits or vegetables.

Song-ho began his morning chores. He swept the hut, soaked soybeans for supper, and washed rags in the mountain stream.

As Song-ho squeezed the last rag in the stream, the sound of a bell rang deep in the valley where many *yangbans* lived. *Ding dong, ding dong*. This was the sound of the school bell from The Sodang School!

Ding dong, ding dong, the school bell rang as Song-ho carried the wet rags back to the hut. *Ding dong, ding dong,* the sound echoed in his ears.

As if the bell were calling him, Song-ho followed it deep into the valley.

At last he came upon The Sodang School, surrounded by golden rain trees. The school was more beautiful than he ever imagined. The bell was now still and silent for study time.

Song-ho tiptoed toward the rice-paper door. The shadow of a master giving instruction to a roomful of *yangban* pupils rose before him.

Suddenly, the door slid open.

The master towered over Song-ho in the doorway. He stroked his long, silvery beard. "I am Master Min. What brings you here, child?"

"I am Song-ho. May I be your pupil?" the boy eagerly inquired.

Master Min looked down at Song-ho in his rags and frowned. "No, that is not possible."

"How can I grow up to earn a good living for my mother when I cannot read or write?" Song-ho begged for an answer.

The boy's bravery brought a lump to Master Min's throat. But rules were rules, and *sangmins* were not allowed to attend The Sodang School.

"Go home, Song-ho," Master Min said, sliding the door closed.

But Song-ho did not budge. He kept his ear to the door and listened to Master Min's lesson.

Little did Song-ho know that Master Min could see his small, huddling shadow through the door! But Master Min was a man with a kind heart. He took pity on Song-ho and allowed him to stay outside during the lesson.

Song-ho learned about ancient kingdoms and great leaders. He learned about The Royal Bee, which was held every spring in The Great Hall at the Governor's palace. Only one pupil from each school across the land would be chosen to compete in this contest of knowledge.

That evening Song-ho spooned soybean soup into a bowl for his mother. She ate her soup as the steam warmed her weary face. "My poor Song-ho! How I wish I could give you more in this world than spotted ears of corn."

Song-ho did not tell his mother about his adventure at The Sodang School. Someday he would surprise her with all that he had learned.

Later Song-ho shucked the spotted ears of corn, thinking: *If I learn how to read and write, I will give my mother golden ears of corn!*

꒰꒱

Every day Song-ho returned to The Sodang School, following the sound of the bell deep into the valley. He would hide behind a golden rain tree until all the finely dressed *yangban* pupils were inside, until the school bell grew still and silent.

Every day the sight of Song-ho's shadow at the door brought a tear to Master Min's eye. Every day he delivered his lesson loud and clear.

Winter arrived. Icicles hung from the bare branches of the golden rain trees at The Sodang School.

Song-ho huddled by the door, bent and shivering. His ears were so frozen, he could hardly hear Master Min's lesson.

Suddenly, the door slid open.

"Come in, Song-ho," Master Min commanded him.

Song-ho stepped into a roomful of *yangban* pupils. They gasped at the sight of the boy in rags.

"Song-ho has been very sneaky," Master Min explained. "He has been listening to our lessons. We must put his eavesdropping to a test."

"Who was the father of our alphabet?" one *yangban* pupil questioned Song-ho.

"King Sejong," Song-ho answered.

"What is the largest island of our country?" another *yangban* pupil asked.

"Cheju Island," Song-ho replied.

After each *yangban* pupil in the classroom had tested Song-ho, Master Min spoke: "Welcome to The Sodang School, Song-ho."

The *yangban* pupils respectfully bowed their heads and chorused, "Welcome to The Sodang School."

❧

That evening Song-ho spooned soybean soup into a bowl for his mother. She had spent her whole day collecting chestnuts from the ground. Now she drooped with despair. "My poor Song-ho! How I wish I could give you more in this world than cracked chestnuts."

Later Song-ho roasted a pan of cracked chestnuts, thinking: *If I learn how to read and write, I will give my mother perfect chestnuts!*

Spring arrived. As the golden rain trees bloomed gracefully at The Sodang School, Song-ho learned how to read books from cover to cover. He learned how to dip a delicate paintbrush into a black inkstone and write beautiful poetry on white scroll paper.

Song-ho became a prize pupil.

ॐ

One morning Master Min asked Song-ho to stand before the class. "You have been chosen by your classmates to represent The Sodang School in The Royal Bee," Master Min announced.

Song-ho could not believe his ears!

Master Min proudly presented Song-ho with a bundle of silk. "A gift from your classmates."

"A gift to wear to The Royal Bee!" hailed the *yangban* classmates. "A gift of good luck!"

Song-ho slowly untied the bundle. Out tumbled a colorful ceremonial costume, sparkling like a mountain of jewels.

Song-ho bowed his head in thanks.

⁂

That evening Song-ho spooned soybean soup into a bowl for his mother. She had just returned from a long day in the melon fields. "My poor Song-ho! How I wish I could give you more in this world than bruised melons."

Later Song-ho sliced the bruised melons, thinking: *If I win The Royal Bee, I will give my mother sweet melons!*

The morning of The Royal Bee arrived!

The Governor's palace stood among mountains that touched the sky. In his ceremonial costume of deep green and shimmering pink, Song-ho walked with Master Min through the iron gates. They entered The Great Hall.

Master Min escorted Song-ho to a large gathering of *yangban* pupils who stood before a panel of judges. Then Master Min took his place in the audience.

A hush came over the palace as the Governor made his entrance with the help of a pearl-studded cane. From his royal seat he proclaimed: "Welcome to The Royal Bee! The judges will test you from their Book of Knowledge. A wrong answer and you will fall out of the contest. When The Royal Bee is over, only one pupil will remain standing— the number one pupil in the land!"

One by one the pupils were asked questions by the panel of judges. One by one the pupils began to fall out of The Royal Bee.

Hours later, only two pupils remained. One of the pupils was Song-ho!

"What mountain has twelve thousand rocky peaks?" one judge questioned Song-ho.

"Diamond Mountain," Song-ho answered.

"What Far East country borders Korea?" another judge asked the *yangban* pupil.

"China," the *yangban* pupil replied.

The Royal Bee went on and on.

ॐ

Darkness fell over the palace. The audience grew restless, and the judges ran out of questions.

Finally, the Governor stood up and spoke: "There is only one way to decide the winner of The Royal Bee. Each of you must answer this question: What does winning The Royal Bee mean to you? When the moon shines into The Great Hall, you must deliver your answer."

When the moon shone in The Great
Hall, the *yangban* pupil stepped forward.
"I have studied all year long to compete
in The Royal Bee, Great Governor. If I win
I will follow in my ancestors' footsteps. I
will attend the finest schools and grow up
to be a famous scholar!"

The audience clapped politely.

Now it was Song-ho's turn. He took a nervous step forward and began to speak:

My mother works in the fields
Every day from dawn to dusk,
Knowing in her heart there is
No hope for people like us.
Then Master Min took me in
And broke the honored rule.
He let a sangmin *boy like me*
Attend The Sodang School.
He taught me how to read and write—
And I am at The Royal Bee!
The gift of hope has now been won
For my poor mother and me.

Like the full moon, silence filled
The Great Hall.

Then the audience rose to its feet and clapped so thunderously that The Great Hall seemed to shake! Master Min shed tears of joy as the Governor declared Song-ho the winner of The Royal Bee.

"You have shown great courage by speaking the truth, Song-ho," the Governor stated.

A royal ceremony followed. The Governor presented Song-ho with a prize cow draped with silk and a necklace of glittery gold coins.

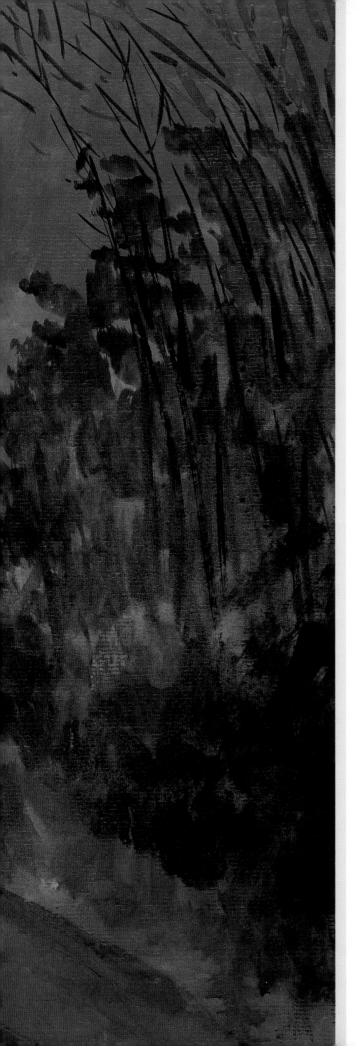

The hour was late when Song-ho made his journey home with his prize cow. Across the mountains he could hear his mother calling him.

"Song-ho! Song-ho! Where are you?"

Tonight Song-ho would surprise his mother with all that he had learned at The Sodang School. And how he had won The Royal Bee! And a prize cow! And silk! And gold coins!

Just then the sound of a bell rang deep in the valley. *Ding dong, ding dong.* This was the sound of the school bell from The Sodang School. In honor of Song-ho! *Ding dong, ding dong,* the school bell rang as Song-ho hurried back to the hut. *Ding dong, ding dong,* the sound echoed in his ears.